Christa Kempter was born in Ingelheim, Germany, and since 1995 she has worked as a freelance children's author for radio and television. She previously wrote the well-known book *Wally and Mae*. Bear, published by NordSüd Verlag. Her favorite subjects are the small miracles that occur in everyday life, and she is delighted when now and then a little dream comes true.

Amélie Jackowski was born in Toulon, France, and studied at the École des arts décoratifs in Strasbourg and the University of Aix-en-Provence. Her best-known picture book, *The Bad Mood*, has long been one of NorthSouth's best sellers and has been translated into more than ten languages. Today Amélie works in France as a freelance illustrator of children's books, and she regularly contributes to exhibitions.

Copyright © 2020 by NordSüd Verlag AG, CH-8050 Zürich, Switzerland.
First published in Switzerland under the title *Doktor Maus*.
English text copyright © 2020 by NorthSouth Books, Inc., New York 10016.
Translated by David Henry Wilson.
All rights reserved.
No part of this book may be reproduced or utilized in any form or by any means, electronic or mechanical, including photo-copying, recording, or any information storage and retrieval system, without permission in writing from the publisher.
First published in the United States, Great Britain, Canada, Australia, and New Zealand in 2020 by NorthSouth Books, Inc., an imprint of NordSüd Verlag AG, CH-8050 Zürich, Switzerland.
Distributed in the United States by NorthSouth Books, Inc., New York 10016.
Library of Congress Cataloging-in-Publication Data is available.
ISBN: 978-0-7358-4410-0
1 3 5 7 9 · 10 8 6 4 2
Printed in Germany by Grafisches Centrum Cuno GmbH & Co. KG, 2020.
www.northsouth.com

Christa Kempter   Amélie Jackowski

DOCTOR MOUSE

Translated by David Henry Wilson

North
South

Every morning when the sun rose over the forest,
Doctor Mouse opened the old barn door and carefully
hung up his sign:

He then straightened up the six chairs, put on his
white coat, laid three cushions on a wobbly armchair,
and sat down on the top one. This enabled his patients
to see him.

Doctor Mouse did not have to wait long. The first patient to come flapping into the office, looking very nervous, was a chicken.

"Keep calm, Ms. Chicken, keep calm," said Doctor Mouse. "Now sit down quietly and wait. Chair number one, please."

"But the sun rose ages ago!" squawked the chicken.

"Consultations only begin when all six chairs are occupied, Ms. Chicken."

"I've never heard anything so crazy in all my life. *Cluck cluck*. And you've got your coat on the wrong way around, Doctor," cackled the chicken.

"That's the way it is," said Doctor Mouse, and he took a bite out of his cube of breakfast cheese.

Not long after, the second patient arrived: a dog.
"Hello, Mr. Dog. So what's wrong with you?
You're next in line. Chair number two, please."

The third patient was a bear.

"Good morning, Mr. Bear. Chair number three, please."

The fourth patient was a rabbit.

"Come in, come in! No need to be shy. Chair number four, please."

The fifth patient was an owl.

"Up so early, Ms. Owl? Chair number five, please."

Doctor Mouse waited for a while, but chair number six remained empty. "Well, that's a surprise! There's never been a vacant chair before!" said Doctor Mouse. "Never mind, the day is still young. We'll begin the consultations all the same."

"Let's start with you, Ms. Chicken. What's the trouble?"

"It's terrible. I'm all aflutter, can't keep still, and simply can't get any sleep. And it's all because of a dreadful ghost! Every night it sits under my bed moaning and groaning until my head's bursting!"

"But Ms. Chicken, there is no such thing as a ghost," said Doctor Mouse.

"Of course there is! I've seen one with my own eyes!"

"No problem, Ms. Chicken," said Doctor Mouse. "We'll find a way to deal with it. I just need to have a little think. Let's move on for now."

"I don't think I know you, Mr. Dog."

"Of course you know me, Doctor Mouse," snapped the dog.
"I come to your office every week."

"If you say so, then it must be true," replied Doctor Mouse.
"So why have you come this week?"

"I've told you a hundred times. I get bored at home. At least
I can have a bit of company here."

Even before the doctor could say anything, the chicken let
out a happy squawk. "Then you need a friend. Someone like me."

The dog looked at the chicken in surprise. "You think so?
Yeah, well, okay. You can be my friend, and I'll chase your
ghost away for you."

"Excellent!" cried Doctor Mouse. "I think that solves the
problem."

"Now we come to you, Mr. . . . um . . . Wolf. How are your stomach pains today?"
"Bear, not Wolf," growled the bear. "And my stomach is still hurting."

"What do you normally eat for breakfast?"
asked the doctor.

"Cream cake."

"And for lunch?"

"Cream cake."

"And for supper?"

The bear thought for a moment. "Cream cake.
There is nothing better in the whole world. Would
you like to try a piece?"

He pulled out a packet and held a piece of cream
cake under Doctor Mouse's whiskers. But the doctor
preferred to stick with his cube of cheese.

"We'll soon find a cure for you, Mr. Bear, but let's
have a look at our next patient first."

"Now then, Ms. Rabbit, what's the matter with you? Your cheeks are bright red!"

Ms. Rabbit shuffled awkwardly back and forth on her chair. "That *is* the problem," she whispered. "I'm just so shy. That's why I keep going red."

"But it suits you, Ms. Rabbit," said the bear.

"Really?" said Ms. Rabbit, turning even redder. "Besides, I'm much too small. Nobody ever takes any notice of me."

"That's not so good," said the bear. "A nice little rabbit like you. Listen, I've got an idea. If the two of us go out together, everybody's going to think: she must be a mighty fine rabbit to have such a great big bear for a friend! And if we go through the town on my motorbike together, they'll all be amazed at how brave you are."

"That would be lovely," whispered the rabbit. "And I could cook you a nice healthy meal of carrot soup, with dandelion dumplings and lots of mint tea."

The bear wrinkled his nose. "But we'll have cream cake for after."

"Not too much, though," warned Doctor Mouse, shoving another piece of cheese into his mouth. These consultations were hard work, and they made him hungry. "Wonderful! Another case solved!" he said, with his cheeks bulging.

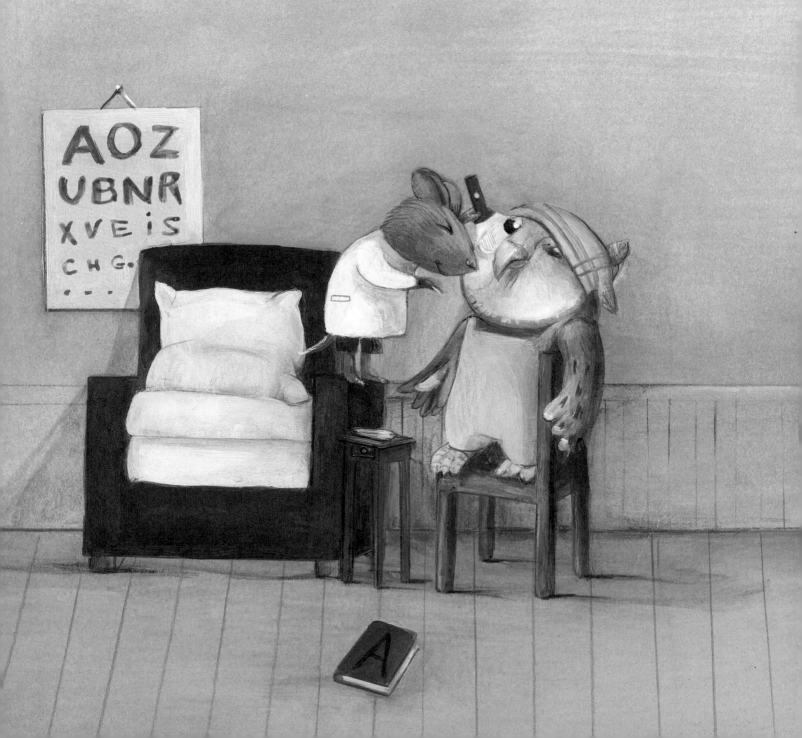

"Your turn now, Ms. Owl. Tell me all your troubles."

"Something's not right with me, Doctor Mouse. The day before yesterday, I didn't recognize my cousin at the top of the pine tree. Yesterday I flew straight into a tree trunk. And even you look rather blurred as well."

Doctor Mouse shined his light into the owl's eyes. "It may be, Ms. Owl, that you are in need of a pair of spectacles."

"Spectacles?" screeched the owl. "I never thought of that!"

At this moment a fox came strolling in. "What are you all doing here?"

"At last!" cried Doctor Mouse, clapping his feet with pleasure. "The sixth patient. Chair number six, please."

"What do you mean, patient?" asked the fox. "I've just popped in for a short rest, and also because I'm hungry. Every day I run up and down the mountain three times."

"Please don't overdo it, Mr. Fox," warned Doctor Mouse. "Once up and down the mountain is all you need to stay healthy. And now, would you all please keep quiet!"

The somewhat startled fox bowed his head.

The bear generously pushed the last cream cake toward the fox, who was delighted.

"I've also brought something nice with me," said the fox. Out of his backpack he took an alarm clock, a sun hat, a glove, and a pair of spectacles.

"Ah, a pair of spectacles for Ms. Owl!" cried Doctor Mouse triumphantly.

"Well, fancy that!" screeched Ms. Owl. "I don't believe it!
I can see every hair of your whiskers, Doctor Mouse! And every
feather on Ms. Chicken! May I keep the spectacles, Mr. Fox?"

"Of course you can," said Mr. Fox. "They're of no use to me."

Out of sheer joy, Ms. Owl kissed Mr. Fox on the cheek.

"Ouch!" howled the fox. "With a beak as sharp as that,
you shouldn't kiss anybody!"

Doctor Mouse giggled, and gobbled up his last cube of cheese.

"Isn't it wonderful, my dears? Everybody fit and well again, all bright and cheerful!" He yawned. His little eyes became even smaller, and very soon he was happily snoring away in his armchair. Very quietly the animals left the barn.

But no sooner were they outside than they started running and racing, flapping and fluttering around.

"He's SO nice!" said the dog.

"Best doctor in the world," boomed the bear. "He always knows what to do."

"It's just a pity he wears his coat the wrong way around," clucked the chicken. "I'll have to come again tomorrow. Otherwise, who's going to tell him?"

It would be some time before the sun set behind the forest. But if no more patients came, Doctor Mouse would simply be able to go on sleeping. After all, tomorrow was sure to be another busy day.